I'm Going to be a Big Brother!

LINDSEY COKER LUCKEY

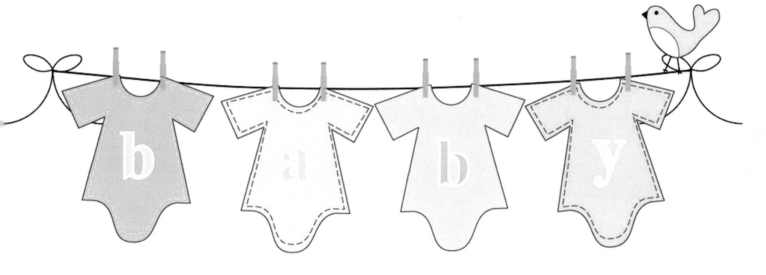

I'm going to be a big brother
And I don't know what to think
Will Daddy get rid of all of my toys?
Or paint my bedroom pink?

I'll have to share my
Mommy
It won't be just us
three.
But will she love that
baby,
Just as much as she
loves me?

Mommy's tummy is growing.
It's getting bigger every day.
That means the baby will be here soon
Will I still be able to play?

Mommy and Daddy,
Will they have time for
me?
Will I be all alone?
Will they ever be free?

The baby is here!
I am a big brother!
I am so happy,
I love the baby like no other!

I want to share my toys,
And share my attention too!
I want to play with that baby
And be a best friend too!

I CAN still play
And I can keep all of
my toys!
Mommy and Daddy
still love me,
Oh boy, oh boy!

Now I have a best friend
for life
I can teach the baby
How to crawl, talk,
and ride a bike!

Made in United States
Troutdale, OR
10/24/2023

13952498R00017